Nate the Great
and the
Big Sniff

Nate the Great
and the
Big Sniff

by Marjorie Weinman Sharmat
and Mitchell Sharmat
illustrated by Martha Weston
in the style of Marc Simont

A YEARLING BOOK

This is a work of fiction. Names, characters, places, and incidents either are the
product of the author's imagination or are used fictitiously. Any resemblance to
actual persons, living or dead, events, or locales is entirely coincidental.

Text copyright © 2001 by Marjorie Weinman Sharmat and Mitchell Sharmat
Cover art and interior illustrations copyright © 2001 by Martha Weston
New illustrations of Nate the Great, Sludge, Fang, Annie, Rosamond, and
Claud by Martha Weston based upon the original drawings by Marc Simont.
Extra Fun Activities text copyright © 2007 by Emily Costello
Extra Fun Activities illustrations copyright © 2007 by Laura Hart

All rights reserved. Published in the United States by Yearling, an imprint of
Random House Children's Books, a division of Penguin Random House LLC,
New York. Originally published in hardcover in the United States by Delacorte
Press, an imprint of Random House Children's Books, in 2001, and subsequently
published in paperback with Extra Fun Activities by Yearling, in 2004.

Yearling and the jumping horse design are registered trademarks of
Penguin Random House LLC.

Visit us on the Web! randomhousekids.com

Educators and librarians, for a variety of teaching tools, visit us at
RHTeachersLibrarians.com

Library of Congress Cataloging-in-Publication Data is available upon request.
ISBN 978-0-385-32604-9 (trade) — ISBN 978-0-385-90020-1 (lib. bdg.) —
ISBN 978-0-440-41502-2 (pbk.) — ISBN 978-0-307-55843-5 (ebook)

Printed in the United States of America
36 35 34 33 32 31

First Yearling Edition 2003

Random House Children's Books supports the First Amendment and
celebrates the right to read.

For our sweet, shaggy

DUDLEY SHARMAT
a.k.a.
DUDS
DIPSEY DOODLE
and
COMPUTER DOG

December 3, 1988 (adopted)–March 3, 1997

—M.W.S.

—M.S.

For Diane and Nancy, my good friends

—M.W.

Chapter One
The Long Wait

My name is Nate the Great.
I am a detective.
My dog, Sludge, is a detective too.
Today I had my biggest case ever.
But Sludge couldn't help me.
Because looking for Sludge
was the case!
Sludge was missing.
Lost. Gone.
I had to find him!
This morning Sludge and I
went out to shop.
We went to my favorite store,
Weinman Brothers.
Sludge isn't allowed in stores.

I go in and Sludge waits outside.
Sludge is great at waiting.
He likes to watch people go by.
He always finds a few
he likes to sniff.
"I am going to buy one thing,"
I said to Sludge.
"I will be right back."
Sludge wagged his tail
and sat down.

I walked into the store.

I was looking for a present for Sludge.

I went straight to the pet department.

I found a nice dog bowl.

And a long line of people.

They were all waiting to buy things.

I went to the end of the line.

Then I, Nate the Great, counted.
I was waiter number twenty-one.
I could grow old waiting in this line.
The seasons could change.
The world could change.
Pancakes could disappear.
And Sludge would still be waiting.
I put down the bowl.
I walked away. I went outside.

Sludge was gone!

Chapter Two
Slippy Sloppy Dog

I looked for Sludge.
I saw big puddles.
The air smelled of rain.
"Sludge!" I called.
"Woof!"
I heard a dog's bark.
I turned around.

Annie and her dog, Fang,
were standing there.
Fang is big and scary.
Today his teeth were wet
and gleaming.

"Are you looking
for Sludge?" Annie asked.
"I saw him sitting out here.
It started to rain.

Sludge got wet and drippy
and sloppy.
He moved closer to the store."
"So where is he?" I asked.
Annie pointed.
"He sat down on the thing
that opens the store door," she said.
"The door opened.
Sludge looked surprised.
He walked into the store."
"He walked *in*?" I asked. "Then what?"

"Sludge shook himself off.
He sat down and waited.
For you, I guess.
A saleslady came over with a towel.
She started to wipe him off.

Then another saleslady
yelled at him,
'You're not a shopper.
You have no money.
Leave!'
She grabbed Sludge.
But he slipped away.
'You slippy sloppy dog!'
she yelled after him."
"Then what happened?" I asked.

"Sludge ran into
the hat department.
I couldn't see him anymore.
So Fang and I went after him.
But the mean lady stopped us.
She looked at Fang and said,
'Too many teeth. Bad breath.
And no money. *Out!*'"
"Then what?"
"Fang growled at her.
She screamed and stepped back.

I took Fang outside.
A minute later you came along.
You missed Sludge."
"I must go to the hat department," I said.
"Fang and I will wait here," Annie said.
"In case Sludge comes back outside."
"He'd have to pass that lady,"
I said. "Sometimes Sludge is brave.
But not that brave."
"Well, Fang is.
He can go back in and get Sludge
past that lady.
He and I will guard the door.
If we get Sludge, we will find you."

Chapter Three
Hats and Underwear

I, Nate the Great,
rushed back into the store.
Annie called after me,
"Don't forget:
Sludge looks slippy sloppy.
It could be a clue."

I went to the hat department.
There were hats
of every size and shape.
But I did not see Sludge.
I looked for wet pawprints.
Perhaps there was a trail.
Nothing.
I went up to a salesman.
"There was a wet dog . . . ," I began.

The man pointed to the left.

"That way," he said.

I rushed to the underwear department.

No Sludge.

Could he be hiding from that mean lady?

But where could he hide?

I saw a sign: DRESSING ROOMS.

I did not want to peek into those rooms.

I did not want to look at underwear
with anyone inside it.

But I had to find Sludge.

I went to the dressing rooms.

"Sludge!" I called.

Somebody peeked out
from a dressing room.

Somebody who looked strange.

Very strange.

It was Rosamond.
She was wearing a nightshirt
that had MEOW
printed across the front.
It was much too small for her.
"I'm shopping," she said.
"This is for my cat Big Hex.
I buy all my cats' clothes here."

"Have you seen Sludge?" I asked.
"Yes," she said. "I saw him run
in and out of this department.
I don't blame him.
There's not a thing here for dogs."
"Thank you for that information," I said.
I left.
Where could Sludge have gone?

Chapter Four
Lost!
My Best Friend!

I needed clues.

I needed pancakes.

I always eat pancakes

when I can't solve a case.

They help me think.

I knew there was a cafeteria

at the back of the store.

They serve great pancakes.

But I did not want to go there.

I was not hungry.

I was sad.

I was thinking about Sludge.

How I had first met him.

In a field.

How he had become my dog.

And my best friend.

And now he was lost.

I went to a pay phone.

I called home.

The answering machine came on.

I left a message for my mother.

Dear Mother,
I am on my biggest
case. Sludge is lost.
I will be back. I hope
Sludge will be too.
Love,
Nate the Great

I hung up.
Where should I look next?
In this big store, who would know
where Sludge might be?
Of course!
I, Nate the Great, rushed to
the lost and found department.

Chapter Five

On the Run

I saw somebody I knew.

It was not Sludge.

It was Claude.

Claude spends a big part
of his life in lost and found.

The lost part.

Claude is always losing things.

I went up to him.

"I have lost Sludge," I said.

"I saw him," Claude said.

"Where?"

"At your house on Sunday," Claude said.

"He wasn't lost then," I said.

"Oh, right," Claude said.

Claude pointed to a man

sitting at a desk.

"He knows what's lost

and what's found.

Talk to him."

I rushed over to the man.
I said, "I, Nate the Great,
have lost my dog, Sludge,
in this store."
"Oh, the dog," the man said.
"We know about him.

He's been spotted
all over the place.
Nobody who sees him
will ever forget him,
I'll tell you that.
But we can't catch him.
He just runs and runs.
I haven't had a report
for five minutes.
He could be anywhere."

"Runs and runs?" I said. "Hmm."

"Hmm, what?" the man asked.

"A clue," I said.
I walked away.

Chapter Six

The Tip of a Tail

Sludge could be tired
by now, I thought.
Nobody has seen him
run for five minutes.
I rushed to the bed department.
It was full of beds.
A great place to rest!

I looked on the beds
and under them.
I looked for dog hairs
and pawprints.
And a dog.
Suddenly I saw what looked like
the tip of a tail!

It was under a bed.
Was I dreaming?
Was I hoping too hard?
I got closer.
It *was* a dog's tail!

And it was attached to Fang.
Fang crawled out
from under the bed.
Annie came running.
"There you are, Fang!" she yelled.
"What's Fang doing
in the store?" I asked.

"I thought I saw Sludge,"
Annie said. "So I ran inside.
Fang followed me."
"You saw Sludge?" I asked.
"No. It was a mistake.
It was a wet mop.
But don't worry.
I left the door guarded.
Rosamond came along.
She's standing there
with a big whistle."

"A whistle?"
"Yes. She said every guard
should have one."
I sat down on a bed.

"So Fang is the dog
who's been running
around the store," I said.
"And scaring the customers,"
Annie said.

I, Nate the Great, was sunk.
I should have guessed
that the running dog was Fang!
The man said that nobody
who saw him would ever forget him.
I should have known that was a clue.
The kind of clue I did not want to hear.

Chapter Seven
Think Like a Dog

Annie and Fang left.
I, Nate the Great,
lay down on the bed.
I was tired.
I had used my feet too much.
And my head too little.
I had to think.
Where would a *dog* go
in this store?
Suddenly I had the answer.

Kibbles, leashes, bowls,
doghouses, bones.
Where the good stuff was.
I rushed back to
the pet department.
I counted eleven people
still in line.
But Sludge wasn't one of them.
I went to the dog food.
No Sludge.
I went to the dog toys.
No Sludge.

I went to the doghouses.

Maybe Sludge would be asleep inside.

I looked in every one of them.

No Sludge.

Maybe Sludge had been here and left.

I walked up to the head of the line.

"Excuse me," I said

to the man behind the counter.

"I am in a hurry.

I am on a big case.

I am looking for a wet dog.

A slippy sloppy dog."

"A slippy sloppy dog?" he said.

"And it has a tail, right?"

I nodded.

"Fur?"

"Of course."

"And it barks?"

"Yes."

The man chuckled.

"Nice try," he said.

"But if you want to buy something
you have to go to the end of the line.

I remember you when you were
number twenty-one."
I, Nate the Great, walked away.
I sat down on a dog mat.
This was my most important case.
And I could not solve it.
Sludge always helped me
with my cases.

But now *he* was the case.
He could not help me.
Or could he?
Sludge was a great detective.

Was he trying to find *me*?
Was he sniffing
all over the store?
No. He was afraid the mean lady
would get him.
He had to hide.
But he had to find me too.
How could he do both things?
Suddenly I, Nate the Great,
had the answer.
Suddenly I knew where
Sludge had to be.

Chapter Eight

A Flour Trail

I rushed to the back of the store.

To the cafeteria.

Where the pancakes are.

People were sitting and eating.

There was a room

behind the cafeteria.

There was a trail of flour

going in and out of the room.

It was a trail of white pawprints.

The door of the room
was partway open.
I looked around.
No one was watching me.
I crept into the room.

It was a storeroom.
There were boxes and cans
and jars and sacks.
Sitting on a torn sack
of flour . . . was Sludge!

He was sniffing.

He rushed toward me.

He gave me a big sniff.

Then he wagged his tail.

And licked me all over.

"Sludge, you are a
great detective," I said.
"You knew I had a case to solve.
You knew I always eat pancakes
to help solve a case.
So you sniffed out
this pancake place
and you sat and waited.
You knew you could sniff me from your
hiding place when I showed up.
And that's what you did."
Sludge looked proud.
This had been *his* biggest case too.
I looked at the trail
of flour pawprints.
Did Sludge leave it on purpose?
Or did it just happen to happen?
I would never know.

But I didn't care.
I only cared that
I had found Sludge.
Or he had found me.
Whatever.
I said, "We both deserve
a treat. Wait here."

I went back to the cafeteria.
"Five pancakes to go," I said.
"And a bone."
I, Nate the Great,
and Sludge
sat on the torn sack of flour
and ate the best meal
we had ever had.

～Extra～
Fun Activities!

We ♥ Sludge!

What's Inside

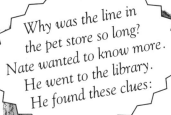

Why was the line in the pet store so long? Nate wanted to know more. He went to the library. He found these clues:

NATE'S NOTES:
Shopping for Your Dog

In 2005, Americans spent about $36 billion on stuff for their pets. That's a lot of money. It's more than we spend on candy ($24 billion) or toys ($20 billion).

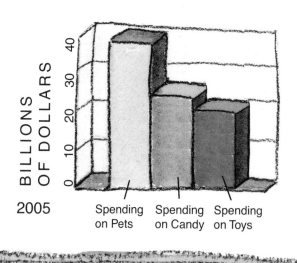

BILLIONS OF DOLLARS

2005 — Spending on Pets — Spending on Candy — Spending on Toys

In one year, the average dog owner spends about $1,571 for basics like food, grooming, and visits to the vet.

Cats don't cost as much. The average cat owner spends about $948 per year on his or her pet. Cats are smaller than dogs. They don't eat as much food. They also groom themselves.

Most dog owners buy more than just basic stuff. About one quarter of all dog owners give their pets birthday presents, and more than half give their dog presents on holidays!

NATE'S NOTES:
Lost and Found Files

Nate isn't the only owner who ever lost his dog.
Each year, millions of pets are lost.
Here is one pet owner's story:

In 2004, Kim Guenther was working at an animal shelter. That's a place for lost or homeless pets. She met an adorable dog there. He'd been abandoned twice. A shelter vet thought he might be very sick.

The dog had surgery. Kim got good news. He would be fine! Kim immediately decided to take the dog home with her. Yippee!

Kim named her new dog Rufus. "Rufus is an affectionate, goofy, and charming dog," Kim said. He also seemed to have a nose for trouble.

One day, after bathing Rufus, Kim put him in the yard behind her building. Rufus slipped out through the gate! Even worse: He wasn't wearing his collar. Kim hadn't had a chance to put it on after his bath!

"I chased after him, but I didn't see which way he went," Kim said. Her neighbors offered to help. They spent two hours searching by car and on foot. It began to rain and sleet.

Kim called the police. She gave her phone number to local businesses. She asked everyone she passed if they had seen her dog. Everyone said no.

Finally, some people told Kim they'd seen Rufus! She searched the area they pointed to. She had no luck. She kept searching into the night.

Eventually, Kim went home. She searched on a lost pet Web site and saw a listing for a dog found close to her house. She called the number listed— and heard Rufus barking in the background! "I can't describe the sense of relief I felt," Kim said. Whew!

Kim did a good job of finding her lost dog.

Here's what you should do if your cat or dog is lost*:

1. First, make sure your pet is really lost. Could he be hiding at home? Look under the beds. Search under the bushes. Maybe he's locked in the attic, basement, or bathroom.

2. Put up flyers around your neighborhood. Include a photo of your pet. Describe her age, breed, personality, eye color, and weight. Put a phone number on the flyer. (Don't put your name or address on it, though. That may not be safe.)

LOST

"SAMMY"
3 yr old Terrier mix
Very Friendly
Please call 855-2130

3. Organize a search. Get a grown-up to walk around the neighborhood with you. While you're walking, call your cat or dog. Ask people if they have seen your missing pet.

4. Ask an adult to make some phone calls. Contact vets' offices, animal shelters, and animal control. It's a good idea to call every couple of days.

5. Check the FOUND PET listings. Kim found Rufus on www.craigslist.com. Another good site is www.awolpet.com. You can also look for FOUND DOG ads in local newspapers.

*For tips on keeping your pet safe, see pages 20–22.

How to Make a Dog Bowl and Place Mat

Don't waste time shopping for your dog. Make him a bowl yourself. Cats like bowls, too. If you have an extra-special pet (or a messy eater), make him or her a place mat as well.

Ask an adult for help.

Start with the bowl.

GET TOGETHER:

- a new plastic dog bowl
- nontoxic paint markers like Painters Paint Markers

DECORATE YOUR BOWL:

1. Use the markers to write your pet's name on the bowl.
2. Add some decorations like your name, hearts, paw prints, or curlicues. If you have room, include your pet's breed, birthday, or adoption date.
3. Let the paint dry. Look at the markers' package to see how long that will take.

Now make the place mat.

GET TOGETHER:

- a large piece of colored construction paper, about 12" x 18"
- photos of you and your pet
- scissors
- double-stick tape
- cookie cutters in fun shapes like bones (for dogs) or fish (for cats)
- markers
- clear contact paper

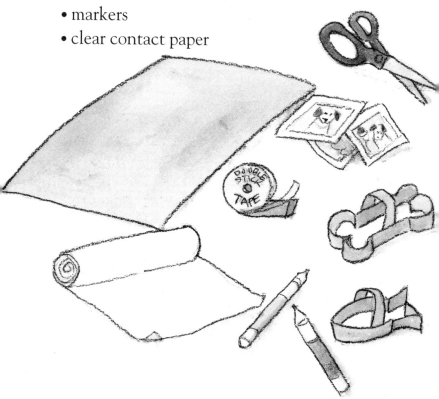

MAKE YOUR PLACE MAT:

1. If you are using photos, arrange them on the construction paper. Remember that you can trim the photos for neat effects.
2. Use small pieces of double-stick tape to hold the photos in place.

3. Decorate the rest of the place mat. Use the markers to trace the cookie cutters. Draw pictures or write words.

4. Enclose the decorated construction paper between two pieces of clear contact paper with the sticky sides facing each other.

5. Trim the contact paper close to the construction paper, leaving a little extra on the sides to "glue" the two pieces together.

6. Put the place mat on the floor. Fill the bowl with your pet's favorite food. Put the bowl on the place mat. Watch your pet gobble his food in style!

Funny Pages

Q: What do you call a flamingo
at the North Pole?
A: *Lost!*

Q: What shivers, looks for clues, and can be
found at the North Pole?
A: *A lost detective.*

Q: What did the peanut say to the almond when he lost his iPod?
A: *Ah, nuts!*

Q: Did you hear about the detective who lost his whole left side?
A: *He's all right now!*

How to Keep Your Pet Safe

Millions of pets are lost every year.
Don't let your pet be one of them!

Stephanie Shain works at the Humane Society of the United States. "The society works to protect all kinds of animals," Stephanie says. Part of her job is teaching kids how to keep their pets safe. Stephanie shared these tips:

• Make sure your pet has a collar and an identification tag. An ID tag is a lost pet's ticket home. Every dog or cat should have an ID tag. Even cats that don't go outside can sometimes escape and get lost.

- Microchips (small computer chips placed under a pet's fur) are a good backup. They contain a code (a string of letters and numbers) that identifies your pet. A vet can read the code with a scanner. Entering the code into a computer tells the vet who owns the animal.

- Never leave your pet alone in a car or yard or outside a store.

- When you take your pet outside, use a leash or a pet carrier. Even calm pets can get frightened outside. This goes for small pets like guinea pigs and hamsters, too.

- Keep a current photo of your pet. It will make finding him easier if he does get lost.

Stephanie lost her cat Miss Boo when she was a girl. "I still think about her sometimes," Stephanie says. "We were very, very sad when we lost her." If you follow Stephanie's tips, that won't happen to you!

More Funny Pages

Q: What always falls without getting hurt?
A: *Rain!*

Q: Rain falls. Does it ever get up again?
A: *Yes, in dew time!*

Q: What goes up when the rain comes down?
A: *An umbrella!*

Q: A man went outside in the rain.
He wasn't wearing a hat or
carrying an umbrella.
When he came inside, not a hair
on his head was wet.
How is this possible?
A: *He was bald!*

Q: What's big and gray and protects you from the rain?
A: *An umbrellaphant!*

Q: What animal carries an umbrella?
A: *A rain deer!*

Q: What did the rain cloud wear under his raincoat?

A: *Thunder wear!*

Kid: Good news! The teacher says we're going to have a test rain or shine.

Friend: What's so great about that?

Kid: It's snowing!

Q: What monster flies his kite in a rainstorm?
A: *Benjamin Frankenstein!*

Q: Can bees fly in the rain?
A: *Not without their yellow jackets!*

Q: What kind of bears like to go out
in the rain?
A: *Drizzly bears!*

Q: What kind of bow is hardest to tie?
A: *A rainbow!*

A word about learning with

Nate The Great

The Nate the Great series is good fun and has been entertaining children for over forty years. These books are also valuable learning tools in and out of the classroom.

Nate's world—his home, his friends, his neighborhood—is one that every young person recognizes. Nate introduces beginning readers and those who have graduated to early chapter books to the detective mystery genre, and they respond to Nate's commitment to solving the case and helping his friends.

What's more, as Nate the Great solves his cases, readers learn with him. Nate unravels mysteries by using evidence collection, cogent reasoning, problem-solving, analytical skills, and logic in a way that teaches readers to develop critical-thinking abilities. The stories help children start discussions about how to approach difficult situations and give them tools to resolve them.

When you read a Nate the Great book with a child, or when a child reads a Nate the Great mystery on his or her own, the child is guaranteed a satisfying ending that will have taught him or her important classroom and life skills. We know that you and your children will enjoy reading and learning from Nate the Great's wonderful stories as much as we do.

Find out more at NatetheGreatBooks.com.

Happy reading and learning with Nate!

Solve all the mysteries with

Nate the Great

- [ ] Nate the Great and the Crunchy Christmas
- [ ] Nate the Great Saves the King of Sweden
- [ ] Nate the Great and Me: The Case of the Fleeing Fang
- [ ] Nate the Great and the Monster Mess
- [ ] Nate the Great, San Francisco Detective
- [ ] Nate the Great and the Big Sniff
- [ ] Nate the Great on the Owl Express
- [ ] Nate the Great Talks Turkey
- [ ] Nate the Great and the Hungry Book Club
- [ ] Nate the Great, Where Are You?

MARJORIE WEINMAN SHARMAT has written more than 130 books for children and young adults, as well as movie and TV novelizations. Her books have been translated into twenty-four languages. The award-winning Nate the Great series, hailed in *Booklist* as "groundbreaking," was inspired by her father, Nathan Weinman. As a child in Portland, Maine, her first job was counting boxes at the real-life Weinman Brothers, a wholesale and manufacturing business owned by her father and uncle.

MITCHELL SHARMAT, a graduate of Harvard University, has written numerous picture books, easy readers, and novels, and is a contributor to many textbook reading programs. He is best known for the classic *Gregory, the Terrible Eater*, a *Reading Rainbow* Feature Selection and a *New York Times* Critics' Pick. He has also coauthored many books with his wife, including the Olivia Sharp series. In Mitchell Sharmat's honor, The Sharmat Collection, displaying the books he's written, was established at the Harvard Graduate School of Education by the Munroe C. Gutman Library.

MARTHA WESTON illustrated *How Will the Easter Bunny Know?* by Kay Winters (Yearling), as well as more than forty books for children, including six she also wrote.